CATCH

A L A D D I N / An imprint of Simon & Schuster Children's Publishing Division * 1230 Avenue of the Americas, New York, NY 10020 * First Aladdin hardcover edition June 2011 * Text copyright © 2011 by Nancy Coffelt * Illustrations copyright © 2011 by Scott Nash * All rights reserved, including the right of reproduction in whole or in part in any form. * ALADDIN is a trademark of Simon & Schuster, Inc. and related logo is a registered trademark of Simon & Schuster, Inc. * For information about special discounts for bulk purchases, please contact Simon & Schuster Special Sales at 1-866-506-1949 or business@simonandschuster.com. * The Simon & Schuster Speakers Bureau can bring authors to your live event. For more information or to book an event contact the Simon & Schuster Speakers Bureau at 1-866-248-3049 or visit our website at www.simonspeakers.com. * Designed by Karin Paprocki and Scott Nash * The text of this book was set in Bikini Bottom Regular. * The illustrations for this book were rendered digitally. * Manufactured in China 0311 SCP * 2 4 6 8 10 9 7 5 3 1 Library of Congress Cataloging-in-Publication Data * Coffelt, Nancy. * Catch that Baby! / by Nancy Coffelt ; illustrated by Scott Nash. — 1st Aladdin hardcover ed. p. cm. * Summary: Everyone from Mom to Grandpa joins the chase when baby Rudy decides he does not want to get dressed after his bath. * ISBN 978-1-4169-9148-9 (hardcover) * [1. Nudity—Fiction. 2. Toddlers—Fiction. 3. Family life—Fiction. 4. Humorous stories.] * I. Nash, Scott, 1959- ill. II. Title. * PZ7.C658Cat 2011 * [E]—dc22 * 2009034934

THAT BABY!

ILLUSTRATED BY
Scott Nash

NANCY COFFELT

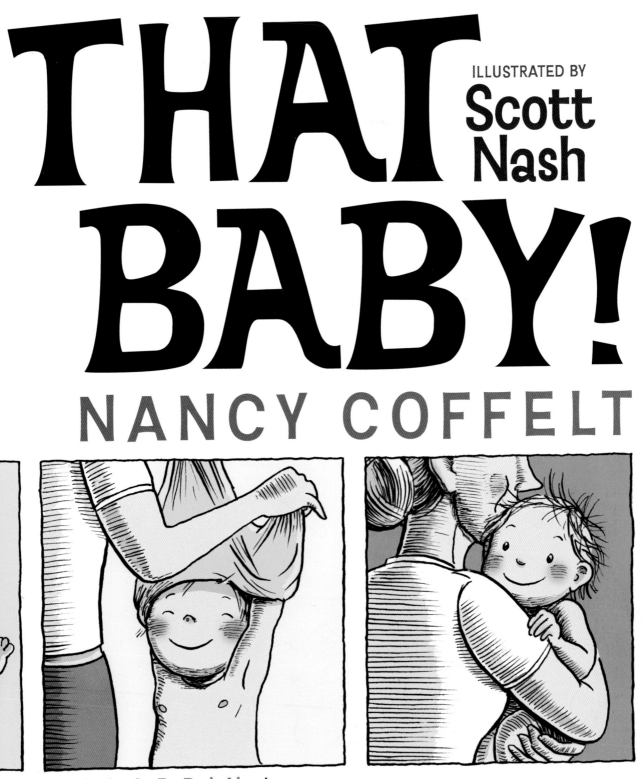

ALADDIN / NEW YORK LONDON TORONTO SYDNEY

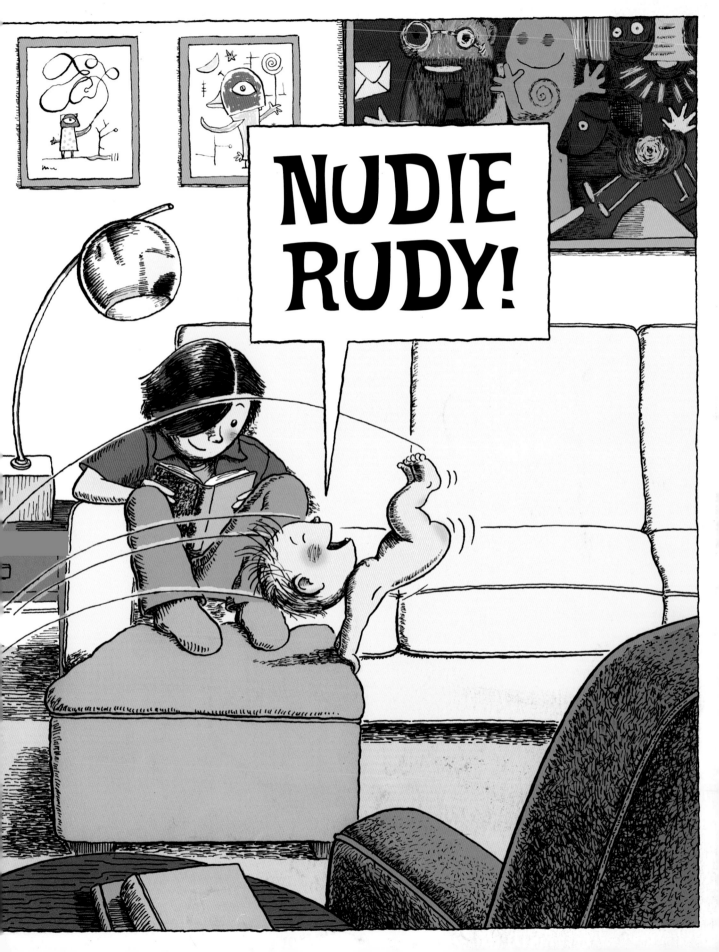

MOM AND BROTHER RUN FAST, BUT. . .

MOM, BROTHER, DAD, AND SISTER RUN FAST, BUT. . .

ARF!

WAIT! HAS BUDDY GOTTEN TO
THE BOTTOM OF THIS MYSTERY?